The KID Is Lost

a novel

by

PAUL KROPP

H·I·P Books

Library and Archives Canada Cataloguing in Publication

Kropp, Paul, 1948–
[Get lost]
    The kid is lost / Paul Kropp.

(New Series Canada)
First published as: Get lost.
ISBN 1-897039-04-2

I. Title. II. Title: Get lost. III. Series.

PS8571.R772G38 2004   jC813'.54   C2004-903732-3

General editor: Paul Kropp
Text design: Laura Brady
Illustrations drawn by: Catherine Doherty
Cover design: Robert Corrigan

2 3 4 5 6 7   11 10 09 08

Printed and bound in Canada

It's a babysitter's worst nightmare: a child goes missing! Kurt has to get help and lead the search into a deadly swamp on his ATV. Will he find the lost child in time?

CHAPTER 1

It Seemed So Easy

The phone rang at ten, an hour too early for a Saturday morning. I opened just one eye and grunted, "Hello?" My voice sounded like I was under water.

"Kurt, do you know where my dumb brother has gone?"

I opened both eyes and sat up. It was Rachel, the girl who lived just down the street – the *hot* girl who lived just down the street. I cleared my throat

3

and tried to make my voice sound sexy – not an easy trick when you first wake up.

"Oh," I said. "Just a sec – I'll check to see if he's playing with Tag."

Outside I heard my little brother, Tag, yelling, "Got ya!"

I rolled out of bed and went over to the window. Tag was down below, and Rachel's brother, Harry, was with him. The two kids were shooting each other with a couple of super soakers. My brother looked he'd gotten the worst of it. Harry looked just as wet. His T-shirt stuck to him like a kid who showered with his clothes on.

"Your brother is outside," I told Rachel, "getting super-soaked by mine." I laughed, thinking of the two little kids squirting each other down below. "Tell your parents that Harry won't need a bath tonight."

But Rachel was in no mood for jokes. "That little jerk gets in more trouble," she growled. "And I'm stuck babysitting him all day. I wanted to go into town, do some shopping and hit the library,

but now I'm stuck here. And as soon as I turn my back, Harry takes off on me."

"I wish Tag would take off on *me*," I told her.

I didn't call my brother "Tagalong" for nothing. The kid has been following me around ever since he was born. You'd think I was some kind of hero in his eyes but what does a six-year-old know?

Then I had a brainwave. I'd been looking for some way to impress Rachel and maybe work up the courage to make a move. Since I was already stuck watching Tag, why not add one more kid? So the words came blurting out: "How about you leave Harry here with me?"

"I couldn't dump him on you," Rachel sighed.

"Sure you could," I said. I was thinking about how grateful she'd be. I kept thinking that maybe, just maybe, I'd score some points with her.

"You don't know how much trouble my brother can be," she said.

"No problem," I answered. "I'm going to be watching Tag while Dad goes out to get some work done on the car. I was going to hang around here and see if I could get the motor working on my new ATV."

My "new" ATV was really a twelve-year-old Polaris that I got from my uncle a month ago, when I turned fourteen. He told me that it needed a little work. He didn't tell me that the whole engine would have to be rebuilt, but I was almost done with that.

I could hear Rachel smiling, even if I couldn't see her. "Well, that's great, Kurt. I could really use some time out of the house. It's been pretty lousy around here the last couple of days what with …" and then her voice broke off. "I'll owe you one, for sure," she said.

"No problem," I replied, trying to sound cool and casual.

"Maybe we can go out for a ride on your ATV later on?" she added. "After looking after my little brother for a day, you'll have earned a little fun."

I really liked the sound of that, as you can imagine. All I had to do was keep an eye on little Harry for a couple of hours. It seemed so easy. How was I supposed to know it would all get messed up?

CHAPTER 2

Where's Harry?

The day was getting hot and sticky by the time I got outside. There was a storm waiting to happen. I could feel it.

Harry and Tag were playing at the far end of the yard now. Just beyond them was the marsh. It stretches from our trailer park all the way to the St. Lawrence.

I always tell Tag there's a scary "bog man" in the marsh, just to make sure he doesn't go out there on

his own. Of course, there's really nothing out there except bugs, birds and mud. But if you're a kid with a big imagination, you can see monsters anywhere.

Tag and Harry were squirting each other and shouting. In the two minutes I watched them, they each got killed four times – and came right back to life. I guess that's what it's like to be a kid.

"Harry," I shouted out.

"I'm not Harry, I'm Battlezoid," he shouted back.

All I could do was shake my head. Here was a

kid named after Harry Potter, the wizard in all those books and movies, and even that name wasn't good enough. "Okay, Mr. Battlezoid – your sister's going into town and I'm in charge of both you kids. Got it?"

"Got it," both kids told me.

I put on an old pair of gym shorts and my blue Freakin' Zombies T-shirt. It's a good band, the Zombies, but that wasn't what was on my mind. Right now, I was hungry so I went to the kitchen to grab something to eat. Eleven o'clock – not quite breakfast, not quite lunch.

My dad met me in the kitchen, looking like a farmer in his old overalls. "I'll be leaving in a few minutes," he told me, sticking his nose into the fridge just as I was doing. "You hear the cop cars last night?"

"Slept right through," I mumbled, pouring the last of the milk on some cereal.

"Trouble down the street," he said.

Trouble at Rachel's? I wondered. *Why hadn't she said anything about it?*

"They ought to throw those low-lifes on the street," my dad went on.

"Dad!" I groaned. My dad thinks he's a cut above everybody else in our trailer park. As far as he's concerned, all the rest of our neighbours are Jerry Springer trash. As if we were that much better.

"It's that boyfriend over there. A guy like that should have been locked up years ago."

"He's not a boyfriend, Dad," I replied. "He's Rachel and Harry's stepfather – understand?"

"Yeah, whatever," he replied. My father never lets facts stand in the way of his stupid opinions.

I left my father grumbling to himself in the bathroom mirror. There was no sense trying to talk to him about Rachel's family. Sure, they had problems, but so did we. At least Rachel and her mom didn't try to pretend they were better than everybody else.

I went off to the shed to work on the ATV. I had most of the thing back together now. I had sanded off the rust, painted the fenders and body parts, and fixed the brakes. Now if I could just get the motor to work so it wouldn't stall … well, maybe Rachel and I would have a really good ride.

I was just getting out a set of wrenches when

Tag and Harry came running in. They were squirting each other – and me.

"Get out of here!" I barked at them both – loud enough to scare them off.

Then I settled into work. A motor is a pretty complex thing, when you stop to think about it. Fuel and air have to mix just right, the spark has to be set just so, and the timing of the whole thing has to be perfect. I had made copies of the service manual at the library, so that was a big help. But still, being only fourteen I didn't know that much about engines. Trying to set everything up right … well, it's tricky.

It was just past noon when I decided to break for a snack. The day was hot – hot and sticky – and sweat was pouring off me like I'd been out in a thunderstorm. Good thing that Rachel couldn't see me like this or I'd never get anywhere.

I went into the house to get washed up. I passed Tag sitting in Dad's La-Z-Boy, watching TV.

At first, it didn't click. I went into the bathroom and soaped up, washing the grease and dirt off my hands. "Where's Harry?" I asked, coming back into the living room.

"When's lunch?" Tag asked.

"Where's *Harry?*" I repeated.

"Don't know; don't care," Tag snapped back.

"Where'd he go?" I repeated, raising my voice.

"Outside, someplace, as if I care," Tag replied. It was as if the only thing on his mind was the show on TV.

So I decided to go outside and shout for the kid. "Harry, you jerk, where are you?" I shouted.

I looked around our place – the parking pad out front and the yard behind us … I even looked under the tarp that covered our old boat.

"Harry!" I yelled again.

No answer. I waited a second, yelled again, then swore to myself. I figured the kid must have gone back to his own trailer.

I went over there, but the place looked empty. I knocked on the metal door, then knocked again. No answer. I was getting mad – how could the kid just take off like that?

"Harry!" I yelled. Then I thought about it for a

second, and figured I should try to be nice. "Harry, come on in, it's time for lunch."

But the only sound that came back was wind blowing over the marsh and a rumble from the clouds overhead.

CHAPTER 3

A Search in the Marsh

I came roaring back to our place, mad as anything. "Where's Harry?" I yelled at Tag. This time I wanted a real answer.

"We had a fight," he said, like it was the most normal thing in the world.

"So why didn't you tell me you had a fight?"

"You were busy working on your ATV," Tag replied, his brain in some kind of TV daze. "Now be quiet – I'm watching *Battlezoids*."

"I don't care what you're watching," I shot back. "Don't you have any idea where Harry went?"

Tag looked up at me for half a second, then shrugged and went back to his show.

This was getting me nowhere, fast. "So what did you fight about anyway?"

"*He* didn't want to play Battlezoids anymore," Tag grumbled. "He wanted to play some stupid computer game."

"So why couldn't you play the stupid computer game or something – something *normal?*" I sighed.

"Dad says that computer games make you dumb," he said, giving me one of *those* looks. Sometimes Tag acts like he's six going on sixty.

"So what happened – did you hit Harry, or what?"

"Well … sort of," Tag said, staring straight ahead at the TV.

"What do you mean – *sort of?*" I yelled, flicking the TV off. "Harry's smaller than you are and almost a year younger – he's only, like, five!"

"I didn't *mean* it," Tag whined.

"But you *did* it."

"Don't blame *me* if Harry's gone," he said. "*You're* supposed to be the babysitter."

I wanted to kill my little brother for simply saying the truth – I *was* the babysitter and I was *supposed* to be watching the kids.

"Okay," I said, taking a deep breath and flopping down on the couch next to him. "Let's figure this out. Think back – when did you and Harry have the fight?"

"Just before *Battlezoids*," Tag told me.

"That's 11:30, right?"

"I guess," Tag said – six years old and the kid still has trouble telling time.

"So Harry's been gone for almost an hour," I said to myself. How was I going to explain *that* to Rachel? I felt as dumb as my dad always says I am.

"Which way did Harry go?"

"How would I know?" Tag said, throwing up his hands.

I wanted to shake him, but I knew that wouldn't help. "Do you think Harry might have gone to the fort?"

"He's not allowed in the marsh, but maybe …" Tag shrugged.

"Well, come on – we have to find him," I said. I headed out the door, pulling Tag behind me.

"But *Battlezoids* –" he moaned, fighting against me as I pulled him.

"*Battlezoids* can come later, you little idiot. First we've got to find Harry."

The marsh was ahead of us, stretching all the way down to the river. It was mostly tall grass and cattails, wet and muddy under your feet, with more mosquitoes than anything else. As the summer went on, the smell of the marsh got stronger. The wind whistled over the bulrushes and carried the smell into our houses – the stink of damp earth and rotting plants.

My old fort was back in there, but the marsh grass was too high for me to see it. The grass was so high that you wouldn't be able to see a little kid like Harry even if he were waving for help.

The worst parts were the swampy sections. If Harry had gotten off a path, into the places where he could sink into the mud … I didn't even want to think about that.

"We're going out to the fort and see if he's there," I told my brother.

"But the bog man," Tag said. He started pulling against my hand, scared to death of going into the marsh. If I dragged him with me, he'd just hold me back, so I came up with a new plan.

"So you just stay here and shout for Harry," I said. Then I started down the path through the marsh grass.

I kept looking for some sign, but there was nothing. Every so often I'd step on a clump of soft

ground and sink into the ooze. Even when I stayed on the path, my foot sometimes sank into the mud up to my ankle.

Behind me I could hear Tag calling out Harry's name. In front of me there was only swamp grass and cattails.

"Harry!" I called. But there was nothing – just the pounding of my own heart and the faint whistle of the wind in the grass.

I reached the fort in five minutes. That's about half the time it usually takes. There wasn't much left of the place anymore. I had built it with Liam Marshall, back when we were still friends. We had dragged wood planks and plywood out into the marsh. Then we had hammered up the shack, painted a skull and crossbones on the door and called the place a fort.

I looked around the remains of our fort, then kicked over some of the wood as if Harry could be hiding underneath. A water snake went zipping into the grass near my feet.

"Harry!" I heard Tag's squeaky voice faint in the distance.

Then silence. I could hear the beating of a million insect wings and a slight breeze blowing over the marsh grass. But there was no human sound out there, no human sound at all.

CHAPTER 4

This Is Getting Serious

When I got back to our trailer, there was still no sign of Harry. There wasn't any sign of Rachel, either – and I was glad about that. I kept hoping Harry would turn up before she did. I kept waiting for the kid to shout, "Here I am," and then we'd start laughing about it all.

But right now there wasn't even a smile on my face. "Okay, Tag, this is getting serious," I told my little brother. "We're going back to Rachel's place and we're going to do a search – a careful search. Understand?"

The kid nodded, his face grim. Somehow he knew that this was getting serious.

I pounded on the door of Rachel's trailer, calling for Harry, with the same results. Nothing. Then I pulled back the boards at the bottom and looked under it, as if Harry would be any place as simple as that. We checked the backyard, the woodpile, the busted swimming pool. But there was no sign of him.

"Let's break into the trailer," Tag suggested.

"What are you?" I asked. "Some little thief or something?"

"No, but Harry showed me how to get in a window," Tag told me. "Maybe Harry's just hiding inside 'cause he's mad at me."

It made sense – so we gave it a try. I boosted Tag up to one of the bedroom windows. He pulled out the screen, then fell into the trailer head first, shouting as he went down.

"Go around and open the door," I called to him.

Tag ran around to let me inside. Then the two

of us went through the place, checking it out like the cops in a made-for-TV movie. It occurred to me that I hadn't been inside here for a long time – not since Rachel and I were kids, back before Rachel's mom married Alan.

Inside, the place was a mess. Rachel's mom was always pretty neat, but this place looked as if there had been a big fight. It made me think of what my father said about the cops coming around last night.

But there wasn't much time to think – only to look. We checked in the closets, under the bed, behind the ironing board. We even looked in dumb places, like in a toy chest, but there was no sign of Harry.

"Where else could he go?" I said, talking out loud to myself.

"Up the street – that's the only other place," Tag answered for me. "Maybe he went to play with the Marshall kids."

Sure he would, I thought. *If he was really mad at Tag, he'd go to some other friend.*

Tag and I walked up the street, checking under

the other trailers as we went. There was no sign of Harry, really no sign of anybody stupid enough to go out on such a hot day. By now, I was dripping in sweat.

The Marshall's trailer was its usual mess when we got there. The Marshalls had four kids, but it looked like twenty from the toys and junk that were all over the yard. Mike Marshall was the same age as Harry, but a jerk – just like his oldest brother, Liam. I knocked on the door frame beside the screen door, then yelled. Mrs. Marshall came to the door with a baby bottle in one hand.

"We're looking for Harry – " I began.

"Kurt, you look upset," Mrs. Marshall replied, jiggling the baby in one arm.

"Well – it's just that I was kind of watching Harry … and now I can't find the kid." It sounded so dumb when the words came out.

"Well, Harry was here a little while ago," Mrs. Marshall said.

I let out a deep breath.

"But he's not here now," Mrs. Marshall explained. "He played with Mike for a little while, and then my guy had to go to his swimming lesson. I thought Harry went home for lunch."

I shook my head – a miserable, cruddy feeling came up in my gut.

"You mean Harry didn't go home?" she asked.

"And he didn't come to our house, either," I told her.

"Well, I'm certain he'll turn up – kids always do," Mrs. Marshall said. "I'll get Liam to help you look for him," she added, going back into the house.

Oh, great. Mr. Bigshot comes to the rescue, I thought. I didn't really want Liam's help. He's a couple years older than me, and ever since he'd started high school, he'd treated me like a little kid. Even now, when we're both in the same school, he acts like he's king whatever and I'm just a dumb peasant.

I was thinking about all that, about how Liam became such a jerk, when Tag tugged at my arm.

"Rachel's back," he said, pointing down the road.

"Oh –" I cursed. I saw Rachel walking up the street toward us, smiling as if it were the nicest day in the world.

"You shouldn't swear, Kurt," my little brother piped up.

"Yeah, yeah, I know that," I said while sweat started dripping down my forehead.

"What are you going to tell her about Harry?"

"The truth, I guess," I said. I wanted to hide or die or climb into my muddy running shoes. How do you say to somebody, *Hey, I just lost your little brother*?

Rachel's long dark hair was pulled back into a ponytail and her face was glowing under the sun. "Hi, Kurt. You get your ATV fixed?" Rachel asked.

"Well, uh, there's a …" I began, but I couldn't find the words.

So Tag broke everything to her: "Harry's lost and we can't find him." He spoke in a stupid, singsong voice as if we were all playing some kind of game.

"What?" Rachel asked. Suddenly the smile on her face was gone and her eyes were staring hard at me.

"Just that, uh, we don't know where Harry went. We … uh … I, well, like, I'm sorry but …."

These stupid words kept coming out of my mouth, meaning nothing, and I felt like an idiot.

Rachel looked at me for a second – confused, or angry, or something. Then she shook her head and groaned, "You mean the little jerk ran off on *you*, too?"

"Well … I guess so," I said. Her tone of voice made me feel a bit better. At least she was blaming Harry, not me.

"Harry and Tag were playing," I explained. "They had a fight and Harry came down here, and then … well, we don't know where he went from here."

"He's got to be around someplace," Rachel said. "He's probably at home – "

"We looked," Tag told her.

"Did you check the fort?"

"Yeah," I said.

"We looked *everywhere*," Tag added.

I hated to agree, but it was the truth. We *had* looked all over – and there was no sign of Harry. The kid was lost, just plain lost.

CHAPTER 5

A Lot of Weirdos out There

That's when Liam Marshall came strolling out of the trailer, looking like he was bored out of his mind. "Hey, man, what's the problem?" he said. Liam was leaning against the door frame, trying to look so cool. "The old lady said you needed my help."

Liam was two years older than me and Rachel. He's the kind of guy who always *reminds* you he's two years older.

"We can't find Harry," Tag spoke up.

"Your little brother?" Liam asked Rachel. He knew perfectly well that Harry was her brother, but must have been trying to make some kind of point. Liam and Rachel had gone out for almost a year when Rachel first began high school. They broke up a couple of months ago. Since then, things have been a little *cool* between them – not cool as in way cool, but cool as in cold.

Rachel nodded. "Kurt was looking after him."

"Oh yeah?" Liam said with a nasty look at me. "And then he goes and loses the kid. Well done,

34

Kurt. Maybe you should open up a babysitting service and see if you can lose a few more brats."

"Ha, ha, *ha*," I said, but I felt like punching the guy out.

"Did you look through all the backyards?" Liam asked, like I was some kind of idiot.

"Of course," I said. "And we checked the trailer and even went to the fort."

"The old fort, eh?" Liam said, looking at Rachel as if the fort should mean something to her, too. She started to blush. I wanted to pound him even more.

"Harry must have really taken off," Rachel said. She sounded worried for the first time, as if this were no stupid game but something serious.

"Well, let's do a really *good* search," Liam said, as if everything I had done was just a waste of time. "I'll go up and down the street, checking with people along the way. Then I'll look through the backyards. Rachel – you go through your place and the places where Harry might play. Kurt – you and Tag go up and check along the highway."

I looked down at my feet and felt stupid. But

I had to admit – it wasn't a bad plan, even if Liam had come up with it.

Tag and I walked up the park road to the highway. It wasn't really a highway, only two lanes of blacktop that led into town, but it was the biggest road we had.

We walked west first, shouting "Harry" into the tall grass beside the road. But only the grass hissed back. A wind was springing up, a strong one, and the weather was turning ugly. You could almost smell the rain coming. Across the road, a German shepherd growled at us as we went by.

We made it as far as George's Variety Store. I walked up to the counter and asked old George if he'd seen a little kid, about five years old, with curly hair.

"You mean Harry?" George replied. "Sure I saw him – real nice kid. Came in with that guy, you know, his stepdad."

My mind made about five forward jumps. Harry came in with Alan, the house was all messed up, Alan had taken off. This was starting to sound like one of those crime shows you see on

TV – a show where the kid always ends up dead.

"When was that?" I asked quickly.

George scratched at his bald head and tried to remember. "About two days ago, I think. Had a two-scoop cone, if I remember right. Lots of ice cream for a kid that size."

I just shook my head. "George, maybe you could keep your eyes open for Harry and call this number if you see him?" I gave him Mrs. Marshall's number, since there might not be anybody home at Rachel's place.

"How long has the little guy been gone?" George asked.

"Maybe two hours," I said, pulling Tag back from the candy shelves. "He and Tag had some kind of stupid fight and then Harry took off."

"Well, Kurt, in the old days I wouldn't have worried too much about that," George went on. "But now – well, there's a lot of weirdos out there, so you've got to be careful. Somebody should have been keeping a close eye on a cute kid like Harry."

Old George was right. Somebody *should* have

been keeping an eye on Harry – and that somebody should have been me.

When we got back to the lane into our trailer park, the first few drops of rain started coming down. Not far away, I could see Mrs. Marshall talking with one of the neighbours. Liam was standing next to them and Rachel was sitting on the steps of the house. Again, there was no sign of Harry.

"I guess they didn't have any better luck than we did," I said to Tag.

But Tag wasn't with me – he was back by the highway.

"Tag, get back from the road!" I shouted as a car went by him.

"Look!" Tag shouted out. He was pointing at something beside the road. "Harry's gun."

It was an orange plastic super soaker.

"Are you sure it's Harry's?" I asked. "There must be a million squirt guns around."

"Sure, I'm sure. When Harry and me were playing, I grabbed it, and it dropped and broke. See," he said, pointing to where the plastic had cracked.

I took the squirt gun into my arms, then turned back down our street. Why would Harry's toy gun be out by the highway?

I could see the look in Rachel's eyes as we came up to the house. I guess she was hoping we'd find Harry, but all we had was a stupid super soaker.

"Any sign of him?" Liam asked when we came onto the porch.

"Just this – Tag found it, up by the highway," I said, holding out Harry's squirt gun.

"By the *highway?*" Rachel asked, her voice starting to waver. "Why on earth would he be up there?"

That was a good question. But the real question was worse – where was Harry now?

CHAPTER 6

The Cops Take Over

I think it was Mrs. Marshall who called the police. The cops seemed to take hours to get there, but Liam said it was only ten minutes. As if Liam would know.

There was no sign of Harry anywhere, and the storm had finally broken outside. Rain was dripping down the windows of the trailer, pounding on the swimming pool cover out back, pattering on the roof of the trailer.

Rachel kept trying to call her mother, but couldn't reach her on her cellphone. Then she tried to track down Alan, her stepfather, but no luck there either. Rachel was on her own. Finally she sat down, buried her face in her hands and started to cry.

I sat next to her and put my arm around her shoulders, but she just shrugged me off. I wanted to tell her how sorry I was, but how do you say "sorry" for something like this? "I'm sorry, Rachel," I pictured myself saying. "I'm sorry I let your little brother …"

And how would I finish the sentence? Get lost? Kidnapped? *Killed?* What had happened to Harry and why couldn't we find him?

I just stared out at the marsh and waited. I kept hoping little Harry would come walking up to us, so everything might be like it was this morning. Back then, I thought this was going to be the very best day of the summer. I thought I was going to score some big points with Rachel. I thought after a ride on the ATV, she'd see me as a really hot guy. Yeah, sure.

"Nice job, Kurt," Liam said to me. It was that mocking voice that I knew so well. "You're quite the babysitter, guy."

"Shut up," I muttered back.

"Hey, don't get all upset with me," Liam went on. "You don't have to explain yourself to me. But the cops might wonder just what you were doing when the kid took off."

Almost on cue, a police cruiser pulled up to the front of the house. Two cops got out, a man and a woman. I had seen the woman cop before, in town, when she had thrown a bunch of us out of the mall. She was a short woman with blonde hair and dark eyebrows. I checked out her name tag – Constable Bailey. The other cop was a tired, older guy whose name tag I couldn't see.

Rachel came rushing out when the cops came out of their cruiser. "My little brother is … I mean, well, we can't find him,"

"You've got to get someone searching along the highway," I added.

But the cops cut us off. "Let's just get a little information down first," the older cop said as he

flipped out a notebook. "Now what is the name of the child who's missing and when did you last see him?"

Mrs. Marshall led us all into their kitchen. The cops didn't seem to be in a hurry. Const. Bailey wanted to know what Harry looked like, when he was last seen and where we had looked.

The old cop started asking Mrs. Marshall questions. It was as if he couldn't be bothered to talk to teenagers, even though we were the only people who knew anything.

The two cops kept going over the same things again and again. I wanted to tell them about the squirt gun, but they were taking it one step at a time. "And you went off shopping, Rachel, while your mother was away?" Const. Bailey asked. It was almost like she blamed Rachel.

"Yes, I already told you that," Rachel said to her. "Besides, Kurt was looking after him."

"But you were working on your ATV out in the shed," Const. Bailey said, staring at me.

What could I say? "Yes, but I could hear the kids playing. I mean, I don't have to be watching them every second, do I?" Okay, I felt kind of guilty, but that was the truth.

"I'm just trying to sort out the facts for the report," Const. Bailey said.

"But Harry's out there – somewhere," said Rachel, looking out the window. "And we're just sitting here talking."

The old cop nodded and looked at all of us. "I think we have enough to get a search started," he said. "I'm going to send for help to cover the area – and make sure that boy's description goes out."

"But there's something else you should know," I blurted out. All this time asking questions to fill out a dumb report and they hadn't given us a chance to show them the one clue we had. "We found something up by the highway – it belongs to Harry."

"What's that?" he asked.

"This super soaker – it's Harry's squirt gun. My brother found it," I said, holding the gun out for them to see.

"How do you know it's his?"

"It's got a crack in the handle," Tag spoke up. "And when we were playing –"

"Harry was playing with a squirt gun like that when he was with my kids," Mrs. Marshall cut in.

That seemed to be enough for the police. By four o'clock, two more cruisers had pulled up in front of the house. The old cop stopped to talk to the new ones. He sent them down the street to begin another door-to-door search.

When he was finished setting up that search – the one we had already done – he came back to us. "Would you two come with me?" he said to Tag and me.

In a minute, the three of us were walking back to the highway. The rain had stopped, but the ground was still wet and the highway was steamy. I tried to remember the spot where Tag had found the super soaker. "I think it was here," I told the old cop. I didn't want to mess up – this time.

"You didn't mark the spot?" he asked.

I shook my head no, feeling stupid. *Why hadn't I thought to do that? Why hadn't I picked it up with a cloth so they could take fingerprints?*

"Are you *sure* this is where it was?" he asked.

"Pretty sure," I said, though everything seemed changed by the rain.

"It was more over this way," Tag said.

The cop turned to Tag. "Stand by the road right where you found the gun."

Tag went over and stood dead still beside the highway. He was pretending to be a statue.

The cop looked at the pavement near Tag, staring at the shoulder of the road. He looked down the park road toward Mrs. Marshall's house. Then he looked off across the road where that noisy German shepherd was barking at us. "You can move now," he told Tag, marking the spot with a big piece of chalk.

"Do you want us to help search for Harry?"

"No," the cop said, "I don't think we're going to find Harry around here."

There was something in his words that made me feel cold, right up and down my spine.

"How come?" Tag asked.

"Well, think about it like this. Would any six-year-old come out to the highway just to play?"

"No," Tag said, "it's not allowed."

The cop nodded and looked hard at the two of us. "So I bet Harry had a reason to come out there. I think maybe he came out to the highway to talk to somebody."

"Somebody in a car?" I asked.

"One minute Harry is out here on the highway," Clark said. "The next minute, the squirt gun is on the road – and Harry is gone."

"You mean Harry's been kidnapped?" Tag cried.

The old cop said nothing – nothing at all.

49

CHAPTER 7

Kidnapped?

No one would ever kidnap Harry for money. Rachel and her family didn't have any. The guy who took Harry didn't want that. He wanted something else ... something worse.

Awful thoughts went through my mind as we walked back to Rachel's trailer. I thought about those kids you see with their photos on milk cartons. I thought about the things that could be happening to Harry. I thought about how stupid I was to let this happen.

When we got to Rachel's trailer, there was a bunch of people waiting by the cop cars. I saw two vans that had TV station logos on the side. I saw a bunch of cops going all over the trailer park while camera crews chased after them.

And then I saw my father talking to one of the neighbours. I figured he was telling him how things like this don't happen to *decent* people. Or how stupid I was to let the kid wander off. Or how stupid I always was. I could tell all that just by the look on his face.

There was a blonde woman standing in front of Rachel's trailer with a mike. I didn't get a chance to hear what she was saying. I was too busy hiding from a guy with a TV camera. It didn't help that Tag was making faces at the TV crew.

At last, we made our way past all that and got inside the trailer. Rachel was there, on the phone. I guessed she was still trying to find her mom or her stepdad. I wanted to do something to make her feel better, but the look on her face told me not to go near her.

So I listened to the cops talk instead.

"Nothing here or on the street," one cop was saying to Const. Bailey. He was with another cop who seemed to be the size of a truck. "We're ready to go into the marsh."

"Two men searching the marsh is enough," the old cop broke in. "I don't think he's out there."

Const. Bailey added, "It seems that the mother called us last night about a family argument. A cruiser came out …" she said, but I couldn't hear the rest of her words.

"That's something," the old cop told her. "My hunch right now is that Harry isn't lost. I bet he went off with someone he knew."

"Harry knew *lots* of people," Tag blurted out. "The crossing guard at school – she's *nice* – and George at the ice cream store. Almost anybody on the street, except that old lady with the mean dog."

The cops gave us a nasty look, like we shouldn't have been talking to them.

I explained, "The kids know most of the people in the park."

"That's not what I'm getting at," Clark said, turning to Rachel. "Your mom and stepdad had a noisy fight last night. What was it about?"

I could tell Rachel felt embarrassed. We pretended not to listen.

"My stepfather was out ..." she began, "drinking, I guess. And my mom had told him, no more of that. So when he came home, she locked the door and ... he tried to get in. He was pounding on the door, but she wouldn't unlock it. That's when she called the police and Alan drove away."

"And your mother went off this morning to find him?" Clark asked.

"I think so," Rachel said, her voice no louder than a whisper. "Maybe she felt bad about locking him out, but she just said she was going off to Montreal. And that she would be back tonight."

"Did your stepdad ever give you or Harry a hard time?" the old cop asked. "Any threats or problems that you can remember?"

I could see what he was getting at and I didn't like it.

Neither did Rachel.

"No," she shot back.

"We ran a check – your stepfather has a record going back ten years," Bailey said.

"That was before … before he knew us," Rachel whispered.

"If we want to find Harry, we have to think about all these things," Const. Bailey explained. "We can't just ignore your stepdad because he seems to be a nice guy. He's taken off someplace, and now your brother is gone. Now I'm not suggesting –"

"So don't say it," Rachel snapped back. "Alan is a decent guy and he's always been great to us. Don't even think about him kidnapping my brother – he just wouldn't!"

And then Rachel started crying. Mrs. Marshall sat down beside her and gave her a hug. She shot a nasty look at Const. Bailey.

Time goes real slow when you're just waiting. The bunch of us sat there, in Rachel's trailer, waiting for news. Outside, we could hear voices from the police and the TV crews. Out in back, there was a dripping sound as water fell drop by drop onto a tin can. Inside, Rachel was crying. Tag was playing on the floor. Mrs. Marshall was trying to be cheerful. It was terrible.

At last, someone turned on the TV. It was six o'clock and time for the evening news.

We were the "breaking news." MISSING CHILD AT TRAILER PARK was the print on screen. There was a shot of Rachel's trailer and then one of Tag making dumb faces. There was a shot of me, trying to hide my face.

Then there was a quick shot of the old cop. He asked anyone who had seen Harry to call the police. At the end, there was a preschool picture of Harry. The kid looked cute, but the picture had to be three years out of date.

Tag was quiet until he saw the picture. That's when my brother burst into tears. He was crying so hard, I thought he'd never be able to stop.

CHAPTER 8

"You're on Your Own"

I took Tag's hand and we went back to our house. "You look awful," my father grunted. He often says cheerful things like that when I'm feeling rotten.

"Kind of how I feel," I said.

I spent an hour in my room, staring at a Limp Bizkit poster on the ceiling. If only I had thought to check on Harry.... If only I hadn't been in such a hurry to get the ATV fixed.... If only Alan hadn't gone out drinking last night. I guess life is full of "if only" stuff. It makes you wish you were smarter, or more careful, or could just do it all over.

I threw some cold water on my face and looked outside. The clouds had cleared and now the sun was low. The sun's light was beaming sideways on the trailers along the street and on the marsh that lay beyond. Harry was out there, somewhere – he had to be.

"Have you … heard anything new?" I asked my father. I was almost afraid to ask, but I had to know.

"No word about Harry yet," he said. "The radio says the police are now holding that guy Alan for questioning. I'm glad the cops finally got hold of that bum."

"He's not a bum, Dad," I said coldly. "He's their stepfather."

"Well, I think the cops are on the right track," my father went on. "It's all pretty simple, really. Alan gets mad at the old lady and grabs the kid to get even. You know how those low-lifes get when the booze hits them. The guy must have been after some kind of sick revenge. He would have

kidnapped the kid one way or another. You just got caught in the middle."

"How do you figure *that*?" I groaned.

My father just pointed at his head, and said, "Just used the old noodle. You can always tell with those kind of people." He looked pleased, as if Harry going missing had proved him right.

I never felt more like slugging my old man than right at that moment, but I held back. I just left him in the kitchen and went into the living room.

Tag was propped on his elbows in front of the TV. There was an empty bag of potato chips on the floor in front of him.

"Who's the suspect?" Tag asked as soon as I sat down.

"How do you know there's a suspect?"

"Someone on TV said the police have a suspect," Tag replied.

"The police think, well, they've found Harry's stepdad and I guess they're asking him questions."

"Why would he kidnap Harry?" Tag asked. "That's *dumb!*"

"Not so dumb," my father broke in. He came out of the kitchen, a beer in one hand and a smoke in the other. "I told you it would be Alan. They're low-lifes, the whole bunch of 'em."

"Cut it out, Dad," I said.

"But it's true," he went on. "The guy couldn't hold down a job to save his life. Then he takes his welfare money and heads down to the bar with it. If it wasn't for your girlfriend's mother, they'd all be on welfare by now."

"She's not my girlfriend, Dad," I snapped.

"Well, I'm glad about that. You can do better than one of them low-lifes."

I couldn't take that stuff anymore – and I didn't care if Tag heard this time. "You are so full of it," I shouted. "So what if Alan's on welfare 'cause he got laid off at the mill? I never saw you turn down the money you get for your lousy back."

"Hey, you just watch your mouth –"

But I didn't care. "What makes you so great – a fat slob who does sweet nothing all day long? What makes *you* so great?"

For a second, my father and I just stared at each other. I wanted to shout more and really let him have it. I wanted to tell him everything that was wrong with him, and us, and our lousy lives. But I didn't. I turned and walked out of the house, slamming the door behind me. In a second, I was walking up the street, away from everything.

It was Liam Marshall who stopped me. "You get in more trouble, Kurt?" he asked.

"No way," I lied, clenching my fists. Liam was the last person on earth I wanted to talk to right now.

"I hear the police picked up Alan," Liam said. "I guess the guy must really be sick in the head, eh?"

"So you believe it, too?" I asked him.

"Why not?" Liam said with a shrug. Maybe that shrug was why we weren't friends anymore. Liam was too much like my dad – too full of his own ideas, too quick to call everyone else an idiot.

"Listen, we both know Alan – we've known him for maybe five years. He's just not the kind of guy who'd do something like that," I said.

"Then why are the police holding him, eh?" Liam replied, so sure of himself.

"I don't know," I said. "But why would Harry leave his squirt gun by the highway if he were going with Alan? It just doesn't make sense."

And then I knew *I* was right – maybe for the first time that day. I didn't care if all the rest of them thought Alan was the guilty one. I *knew* he wasn't. And that meant that everybody else was on the wrong track.

"So what's *your* idea?" Liam asked.

"Well, maybe Harry ran away," I said. "I mean, last night there's a big fight at his house and the

police get called. And then his mother takes off and his sister goes off into town. And then he has a fight with Tag. So the kid maybe feels that all the people who care about him have taken off. Maybe Harry thought he had good reasons for running away," I said, thinking out loud.

"But that doesn't explain why Harry would leave his squirt gun behind," Liam challenged.

"Maybe something scared him," I said, "and he dropped it. Maybe he got scared and ran off – and then he got lost."

"But lost where?" Liam asked.

We both knew the answer.

"There are trails from the highway that go into the marsh," I said, thinking out loud.

"The police already searched," Liam broke in.

"But they didn't do a really *good* search," I said. "Only two cops went out, and they wouldn't know the trials like we do. They wouldn't know the secret trails that we used to take out to the fort and back by the duck blind."

"Hey, don't start looking at me as if I'm going in there," Liam said. "It's almost dark, and those mosquitoes love to eat people for dessert."

"Well, if you haven't got the guts – " I began.

Liam sighed and looked off toward the swamp, shaking his head. "You're crazy," he said, watching the sun set over the marsh grass. "If you want to go out there, you're on your own."

CHAPTER 9

Into the Swamp Again

Liam was dead right about a few things. The mosquitoes were awful at sundown. The police had already been into the marsh. And we didn't know if Harry had gone into the marsh at all.

But he was wrong about something important. I wouldn't have to go into the marsh on my own.

I picked up the phone and punched in Rachel's number, and she answered after two rings.

Rachel sounded as if she wanted a call from someone else – maybe from her mother. All this must have been tough on her. Rachel's brother was lost, her mom couldn't be found, and now Alan was getting grilled by the cops. She had nobody on her side but me.

"I've got an idea," I began. I kept my voice low because I didn't want Tag or my father to hear.

"Did you hear that the police are holding Alan?" she began, her voice sounding both angry and scared.

"I know – and that's stupid," I said.

"I can't believe it!" she went on. "They won't let me talk to him and –"

"Listen," I cut in, "we can't stop the police from doing what they want to do. But I've got this idea that Harry's lost in the marsh. I was doing some thinking and, well, it's the only thing I can come up with. We can't let your brother spend the night out there, alone, so I was thinking –"

"The police already –"

"Yeah, but they don't know the trails that well, not the way I do. Besides, the cops are all hung up on this stupid kidnap idea, so I bet they weren't looking all that hard. If Harry was really scared, he might have tried to hide out on them, too."

"But it's getting dark –" Rachel went on.

I cut her off, "That's why we've got to hurry. There's still enough light to see. If we take the ATV out on the trails, we can cover a lot of the marsh before it gets really dark. With a flashlight, we could keep going until midnight, or later."

There was a silence on Rachel's end of the line. I could almost here the gears turning around inside her brain.

"I'll have the ATV out by the highway in ten minutes," I told her. "If you want –"

"I'll be there," she answered before I could finish the sentence.

I grabbed some coveralls and a sweatshirt, then went out to the shed, trying not to make noise. I needed the big boots and some DEET to keep the mosquitoes away. I needed a flashlight, the big one with the lantern battery, if I was going to stay out past sundown. And I needed helmets, one for me and one for Rachel. I was almost ready to go when

Tag pushed open the door.

"Where are you going?" Tag asked, taking one look at the outfit.

"The marsh," I said in a whisper. "You just keep your mouth shut," I told him.

"I wanna come with you," he whined.

"You're not big enough."

"You don't want me to tell Dad, do you?"

There was no way my father would let me go off to the swamp – not now, not after the way things had gone today.

I thought about clobbering Tag to shut him up, but I knew it wouldn't work. He didn't earn his nickname for nothing. And if he told Dad what I was doing, the old man would send the cops out looking for *us*, too. Somehow I had to explain to a six-year-old why he couldn't come along.

"Listen, Tag," I began. "I know you want to come out and help find your friend, but it's too dangerous. It's going to be dark, the marsh is wet and full of mosquitoes. And Harry might not even be out there."

My little brother was not impressed. I had to think of something better.

"So I've got a special job for you – an important one." My brain was working hard, trying to come up with something for the kid to do. "I want you to keep an eye out your bedroom window. If we find Harry, I'll flash the flashlight three times, like this." I pushed the button on the flashlight three quick times. "If we get in trouble, I'll flash it four times – long, short, long, short. Understand?"

Tag nodded. "And if you get in trouble, do I tell Dad?"

"Right, and get him to call the cops. If you see me flash four times, we need help, like fast. Can you handle that?"

"You can count on me," Tag said, sounding very important. He had a serious look on his face, and I knew he wouldn't bug me anymore to bring him along.

I wheeled my ATV out of the shed and right to the highway before I tried to start it. I didn't want my dad or the neighbours to know that we were going out. Besides, it wasn't legal or safe for us to be riding double out into the marsh. But sometimes a guy has to take a few chances.

The sun was just setting when the ATV's motor roared into life. I climbed on the back, twisted one handle and bounced along beside the road. It was still hot out, and sweat was pouring off me when I met up with Rachel.

"This is a little crazy, you know," Rachel grumbled. We started covering ourselves with musk oil to keep the bugs off. I hated the smell of the stuff, and it stung like crazy if you got it in your eyes. But it was better than getting eaten alive by

the mosquitoes.

Rachel was right, of course. No one in their right mind wanted to go out in the swamp at night. It wasn't just the mosquitoes and sinking into the mud that kept us out. It was a deeper fear. I thought of all the stories we had heard from the time we were small – the bog man of the swamp, the ghost shack, the giant snakes. Of course, I didn't believe any of that stuff anymore. But I couldn't forget them, either.

"Do you really think we might find him?" Rachel asked.

"Yeah, I think we just might," I replied. "And I don't have any better ideas, do you?"

Rachel shook her head and put on her helmet, then she climbed on the ATV just behind me. I twisted the handle and we bounced off the edge of the highway and into the marsh.

CHAPTER 10

The Secret Trails

We raced along one of the secret trails that led into the marsh. This one started by the highway, close to where we found Harry's squirt gun. It led right down to the river.

The path was on pretty dry land and felt pretty solid beneath the ATV. We could have gone faster, but then we couldn't keep our eyes open for Harry.

Ahead of us, the grass and bulrushes had been beaten low. I thought this was a good sign that

someone had come this way, not too long ago. Maybe it was the cops, maybe it was Harry, but I was sure that somebody had walked this path.

"Where does this trail go?" Rachel called out.

"It splits up not far from here," I said. "One path goes to the backyards and the other path leads into the marsh. After that, I think it leads to a shack just beyond Hutch's Island."

"Can we make it that far?" I asked.

"I don't know – I never really followed this one all the way. I guess I believed my own stories about the bog man."

We rode deeper into the marsh. Every five minutes or so, we'd stop and Rachel would shout, "Harry! Harry!" But the only sounds that came back were from night insects and the wind.

Mostly the marsh was bulrushes and swamp grass that cut at your skin like sandpaper. But in some places, the land would get solid and there'd be a small tree and some bushes. We stopped at these, looking at them with the flashlight … just in case. But there was no sign of Harry at any of them. There was no mark, no piece of clothing, nothing.

After about an hour, we got off the ATV to take a break. The noise and bouncing get to you after a while.

It was strangely quiet after riding on the noisy machine for an hour. All we could hear now were the insects and the wind, a hum and a whistle in the night.

"How much farther?" Rachel asked.

"I hope not much," I complained, trying to figure how far we'd come. It was now pitch dark. With luck, my dad would not have noticed that I was gone. With bad luck, he'd probably ground me for life.

"I don't think the shack can be too far from here," I said.

"Harry couldn't have gotten this far," Rachel replied. Her voice sounded tired, like she felt that we were getting nowhere.

"You never know," I said. "If he was scared and confused, he could go a long way – or no distance at all. But we can't quit before we get to the river," I added.

"You're right," she said. "Even if we don't find anything, we at least gave it a try."

The two of us climbed back on the ATV and I kicked at the starter. Nothing. I kicked at it again, praying that it would turn over.

"You're not out of gas, are you?" Rachel asked. "I mean, that would be really stupid."

"No, this is the problem I was working on this morning." I said, mostly talking to myself. "I've just got to jam the air intake...." I really did know what to do, but it was a little embarrassing. I had to get Rachel to kick-start the ATV while I held the mixing valve, but it finally worked. The motor roared and we got going again.

At least, until the trail turned to mud. The rain during the day must have raised the water in the marsh, so now our path was getting soft. The ATV could handle this pretty well, but it didn't have that much ground clearance. So long as we could keep on moving, we were fine. Mud kept shooting out of the tires, but we kept rolling. In the battle of machine versus mud, we were doing pretty well for a while. And then the mud got us, one wheel at a time.

"Can't you do something?" Rachel yelled out.

"I'm trying!" I screamed.

I dropped the ATV into first gear, then tried to slow it way down. If the tires got spinning too fast, they'd just dig right into the mud and make it all worse. But so far, it just wasn't working.

"You'll have to get off!" I shouted at Rachel. "Maybe if I can lighten this up – " I began, but I didn't have to explain it all. Rachel jumped off and got to one side, but not before she got sprayed with mud from the wheels.

I tried rocking the bike back and forth, moving my weight on the seat, but I was getting nowhere. In another minute, the ATV was wheels-deep in the mud and the engine conked out.

I got off the bike and stepped into mud up to my knees. It was so thick and gooey that it felt like quicksand trying to suck me down. Off to one side, I could see that Rachel was covered with mud from her boots to her helmet.

I could just imagine what Liam and my father would say when we came back home, looking like this.

"Looks like the search is over," Rachel said

softly. She didn't even seem all that mad, just discouraged.

"Yeah," I said, feeling miserable. "The search party got stuck. We'll have to walk back and try again in the morning."

I turned and began walking beside the muddy track, back towards the trailer park. Rachel was just behind me, saying nothing. When we turned on the flashlight to see the path, it seemed like a hundred mosquitoes would attack at once. It was better to walk in the dark, using moonlight to see.

We still called out Harry's name, but somehow

the whole thing seemed hopeless. What made me think we could somehow find a missing kid in a swamp, in the dark, all by ourselves? Maybe I'm really as stupid as my dad says I am.

We had been walking for about half an hour when my foot got stuck in some branches. I reached down to free my leg and I felt something cold slither away.

"Kurt –" Rachel said, stopping suddenly.

She didn't say anything, just shone her flashlight beam into the marsh. I heard a noise. Something was moving in the dark.

"What?" I whispered.

I stared into the dark, but the shadows all seemed to be moving.

"Is something there?" I whispered.

Quite a ways off, near a clump of scrub bushes, something was moving towards us. We couldn't see the shape in the dim moonlight, but we could see some creature coming at us.

CHAPTER 11

A Creature in the Dark

I knew Rachel wanted to run, but I couldn't move. The thing was getting closer now, but my legs were frozen beneath me. I was trapped by my own fear.

And then Rachel began running forward into the tall grass. She was running right towards the creature in the dark!

I trained the flashlight on her. I could see Rachel's mud-covered shape when she came face to face with the creature. Then I heard a sound, like a child crying.

It was Harry!

He was alive!

"Is he all right?" I called out as I walked out towards them.

But Rachel was too busy soothing her brother to answer me. "It's okay, Harry, we're here, we're here now."

When I looked at Harry up close, I saw what the marsh could do to a kid. The mosquitoes had eaten him all over. His hands were cut and bleeding from the grass and briars. His face and his hair were caked in mud. And he couldn't stop crying – terrible tiny squealing cries. Even though we'd found him, Harry was still crazy with fear.

Rachel began cleaning the mud off his face. In the light from the flashlight, I could see Harry's face wet with tears. He was cut up and scared to death, but he was going to be okay.

"I was going to run away," Harry told us through his sobs. "But this big dog chased me …" he sputtered.

The barking German shepherd! So Harry had been frightened, dropped his squirt gun, and run off.

"I got lost ..." Harry sobbed. "There were snakes – and the bog man."

"There is no bog man," I explained to him. "It's just a story we made up."

But maybe Harry was closer to the truth than I was. I looked around the marsh and knew this place hated us, that we didn't belong here. The marsh knew we didn't belong, and now it was swallowing my ATV just to prove it.

"Let's get on home," Rachel said to Harry, giving him a drink from her canteen.

"Climb on my back and I'll give you a ride," I offered.

We headed back along the path until we reached a spot high enough that I could see our trailer park. I took the big flashlight and aimed it towards home. Three quick flashes – one, two, three – Harry was safe.

* * *

The cops met us halfway to the park. Tag had told my father after the three flashes, and my father had passed on the word. My little brother might be a real pain, but that night he was one guy I could count on.

Harry had to go to the hospital to get cleaned up, but he wasn't in bad shape. Rachel and I were just exhausted, so we could barely get through all the stuff that the police wanted to know. Sleep came the instant I closed my eyes.

The next morning, I had to face my father right after I got up. He was not a happy guy.

"So maybe I shouldn't have snuck out like that, Dad. But you would never have let me go. And you have to admit, you were wrong about Alan and Rachel's family." We were talking in the living room while Tag watched some dumb cartoon on TV.

"So where *was* the mother?" my father asked. "If they're such wonderful people, where was she?"

"Off looking for her husband," I told him. "What's so bad about that? She called as soon as she heard about Harry on TV, but we were out in the swamp by then."

"Chasing after that Alan guy still doesn't make sense to me," my father said.

"Maybe that's because you don't have any girlfriends, Dad," Tag threw in. "And how come you two are still fighting? It's all over now. Kurt's a hero."

"Kurt can't be a hero – he's a teenager," my dad muttered. "Besides, his ATV is stuck in mud out in the marsh."

"There you go," I answered back, "always putting people down. So maybe I'm not much of a hero, but I did find the missing kid, didn't I? Maybe I messed up by not watching Harry that well, but I found him in the end."

"Yeah, yeah, I suppose," my father said.

"So are you going to admit that you were wrong?" I asked. "Just this once, can you admit it?"

I could tell this was really tough for my father. He pulled out a smoke, hemmed and hawed a little, and finally looked up at me. "Yeah, I guess I was maybe a little bit wrong," he said. "But a lot of people messed up on this one. Maybe you should have been watching the kid, but Mrs. Marshall

didn't keep an eye on him, either. And if the old lady's dog hadn't been loose, well, the kid would never have run into the swamp. And then the cops jumped in and blamed Alan. And that kid Liam, he was as useless as a fifth wheel on a truck. I mean, I wasn't the only guy who made a mistake."

I think my father was going to start a real rant going, but there was a knock on the door. We all looked out the little window and saw Rachel on the step.

"Looks like the hero gets the girl, too," my father said. "Not bad, Kurt, not bad at all."

Here are some other titles you might enjoy:

Student Narc
by PAUL KROPP

It wasn't Kevin's idea to start working with the cops. But when his best friend dies from an overdose, somebody has to do something. Kevin finally takes on a whole drug gang – and their boss – in a struggle that leaves him scarred for life.

Dark Ryder
by LIZ BROWN

Kate Hanson finally gets the horse of her dreams, but Dark Ryder comes with a catch. Kate has just three months to turn him into a winner, or she'll lose her horse forever.

Terror 9/11 by DOUG PATON

Seventeen-year-old Jason was just picking up his sister at the World Trade Centre when the first plane hit. As the towers burst into flames, he has to struggle to save his sister, his dad and himself.

Street Scene by PAUL KROPP

The guys weren't looking for trouble. Maybe Dwayne did pick the wrong girl to dance with. But did that give Sal and his gang an excuse to come after them? The fight should never have started – and it should never have finished the way it did

Hitting the Road
by PAUL KROPP

The road isn't nice to kids who run away. Matt knew there would be trouble even before he took off with his friend Cody. Along the way, there would be fighting, fear, hunger and a jump from a speeding train. Was it all worth it?

Against All Odds
by PAUL KROPP

Nothing ever came easy for Jeff. He had a tough time at school and hung around with all the wrong kids in the neighborhood. But when he and his brother are drowning in a storm sewer, Jeff is the one who never gives up.

Our Plane Is Down
by DOUG PATON

A small plane goes down in the bush, hours from anywhere. The radio is broken, the pilot is out cold. There's only a little water and even less food. Can Cal make it through the woods to save his sister, the pilot and himself?

Scarface by PAUL KROPP

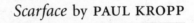

Coming to the United States had been a great thing for Tranh. This was a country of peace and wealth and happiness. So why did Martin Beamis keep picking on him? Did this rich kid have nothing better to do than make life rotten for someone who had already suffered so much?

About the Author

Paul Kropp is the author of many popular novels for young people. His work includes six award-winning young-adult novels, many high-interest novels, as well as writing for adults and younger children.

Mr. Kropp's best-known novels for young adults, *Moonkid and Prometheus* and *Moonkid and Liberty*, have been translated into German, Danish, French, Portuguese and two dialects of Spanish. They have won awards both in Canada and abroad. His most recent books are *The Countess and Me* (Fitzhenry and Whiteside), a young-adult novel, and *What a Story!* (Scholastic), a picture book for young children.

Paul Kropp lives with his wife, Lori, in an 1889 townhouse in Toronto's Cabbagetown district. He has three sons (Alex, Justin and Jason) and three step-children (Emma, Ken and Jennifer).

For more information, see the author's website at www.paulkropp.com

For more information on the books in the New Series Canada, contact:

High Interest Publishing – Publishers of H·I·P Books
407 Wellesley Street East • Toronto, Ontario M4X 1H5
www.hip-books.com